ARNIE
and the Stolen Markers

NANCY CARLSON

VIKING KESTREL

VIKING KESTREL

Viking Penguin Inc., 40 West 23rd Street, New York, New York 10010, U.S.A.
Penguin Books Ltd, 27 Wrights Lane, London W8 5TZ (Publishing & Editorial)
and Harmondsworth, Middlesex, England (Distribution & Warehouse)
Penguin Books Australia Ltd, Ringwood, Victoria, Australia
Penguin Books Canada Limited, 2801 John Street, Markham, Ontario, Canada L3R 1B4
Penguin Books (N.Z.) Ltd, 182–190 Wairau Road, Auckland 10, New Zealand

First published in 1987 by Viking Penguin Inc.
Published simultaneously in Canada

Printed in Japan by Dai Nippon Printing Co. Ltd.
Set in Clarendon Light

1 2 3 4 5 91 90 89 88 87

Library of Congress Cataloging in Publication Data
Carlson, Nancy L.   Arnie and the stolen markers.
Summary: After spending his allowance at Harvey's
Toy Shop, Arnie steals a set of markers.
[1. Stealing—Fiction] I. Title.   PZ7.C21665Ar 1987   [E]
87-6170   ISBN 0-670-81548-9

To the Andersons.
"Remember Saturday mornings
at Harvey's?"

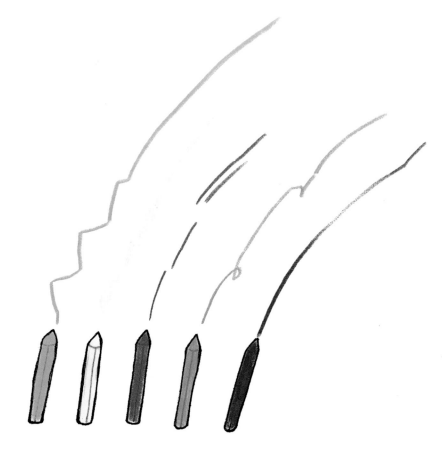

Every Saturday morning Arnie and Louanne
went to Harvey's Candy and Toy Shop.

Arnie always spent all his allowance on candy. But Louanne would pick out neat toys and save her allowance until she had enough money to buy them.

One Saturday, after Arnie had spent every penny on candy, he saw something wonderful!!!

A super-duper marker set, with twenty different colors.

Arnie had to have it!!

He asked Louanne if he could borrow
five dollars.
"No way! I'm saving for a new football,"
said Louanne.

"Boy, is she stingy," grumbled Arnie. "I must
have this set. I could really have fun with it!"

"Hey, Arnie, let's go play!" said Louanne.

But Arnie decided to hang around Harvey's.
"I really, really need these markers,"
he thought.

Suddenly Arnie saw Harvey go into the
back room.

Without thinking, Arnie hid the marker set
under his shirt and ran out the door.

As Arnie ran down the street he bumped right
into Ms. Hoozit.

"Oops," said Arnie.

"Well, how are you, Arnie?" asked Ms. Hoozit.

"J-J-Just fine," said Arnie, and off he ran.

Arnie kept running until he got to his room.
Then he took out all the markers.
"Lucky for me, my mom is out," he said.

Arnie started to get nervous. "I'd better hide these for a while," he thought.

Arnie was a nervous wreck. "I'd better go outside. Harvey may come looking for me," he said.

It was late in the afternoon when Arnie
got home. He nearly fainted when he got
to his room.

His mom had made his bed, and the markers
were sitting right on top!!!

"Where did those come from?" asked
Arnie's mom.
Arnie was going to lie, but it was no use.
"I took them from Harvey's!" he cried.

"I want you to go to Harvey's right now and tell him you stole these markers. You've opened them, so you'll have to pay him back!" yelled Mom. She was *real* mad!

Arnie dreaded telling Harvey he'd stolen
the markers. "I'll probably be sent to jail,"
he thought.

Arnie went in and confessed to Harvey that he had stolen the markers. "Please don't send me to jail," he cried.

"Well, you can work off the price of the markers at the store, every day after school. You can start now. Here's a mop. Get to work," said Harvey.

All week long, Arnie went to Harvey's after school. He worked very hard.

But sometimes it was fun to work at Harvey's. His friend George thought it was neat that Arnie had a real job!

By Saturday Arnie had earned enough to pay
Harvey for the markers.
"You are a good worker," said Harvey. He even
gave Arnie some paper to draw pictures on!

Arnie had no money left for candy. He was
just leaving, when Louanne asked him if he'd
like to play catch.

"No," said Arnie. "I think I'll go home and color with my markers. I've earned it!!!"